2/10

$$\frac{2x}{3-12}$$

CR

Welcome to . . .

THE MAMMOTH ACADEMY

BY TUSK AND TRUNK

THE MAMMOTH
ACADEMY
in TROUBLE!

NEAL LAYTON

Henry Holt and Company · NEW YORK

Henry Holt and Company, LLC
Publishers since 1866
175 Fifth Avenue
New York, New York 10010
www.HenryHoltKids.com

Library of Congress Cataloging-in-Publication Data
Layton, Neal.
Mammoth Academy in trouble! / Neal Layton.—1st American ed.
p. cm.
Summary: As Mammoth Academy spends a term excitedly preparing
for its Founder's Fiesta, wild and dangerous animals called humans are
spraying the school's gates with graffiti and threatening the students.
ISBN 978-0-8050-8709-3
[1. Schools—Fiction. 2. Prehistoric animals—Fiction. 3. Prehistoric peoples—Fiction.
4. Wooly mammoth—Fiction. 5. Mammoths—Fiction.
6. Glacial epoch—Fiction.] I. Title.
PZ7.L4476Maq 2009 [Fic]—dc22   2008050264

First American Edition—2009
Printed in June 2009 in the United States of America
by R.R. Donnelly & Sons Company, Harrisonburg, Virginia.

1 3 5 7 9 10 8 6 4 2

For Anne McNeil
—N. L.

OSCAR

ARABELLA

SOME OF THE OTHER PUPILS AT THE MAMMOTH ACADEMY

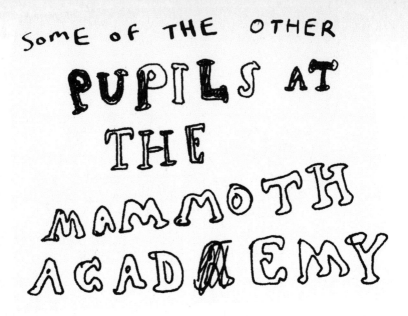

← FLY LIVED IN THE ACADEMY BUT WASN'T A ~~PUPIL~~ PUPIL.

CAVE CAT

ORMSBY

OWL

PRUNELLA

FOX

A FEW MORE PUPILS OF

THE MAMMOTH ACADEMY

ROGER

REMI

RHONDA

REGINALD

REX

RUFUS

REENIE

GIANT
GROUND
SLOTH

CAVE
BEAR

Some of the PUPILS OF The

CAVE
SKOOL

UGH

UGH'S FRIEND

UGE PHINE

UG

PROFFESSOR UGH

Proffessor UGH teaches THE PUPILS OF the CAVE SKOOL

CONTENTS

1.
THE NEW TERM

Oscar was a woolly mammoth, and so was Arabella. They lived a long time ago in the Ice Age.

Oscar and Arabella had been having a terrific time on winter break, romping in snowfields, uncovering secret mountain paths, rooting out mountain berries, and playing Ice Frisbee, but now it was time to go back to the Mammoth Academy.

Dear Student,

The new term starts tomorrow.

All first years must bring with them:

1. Safety goggles, safety gloves, and a safety apron

2. A pair of safety scissors

3. A big pot of glue

4. A big bottle of ink

5. Fourteen lined exercise books

6. Lots of brightly colored material and other things to be
   used to prepare for the Founder's Fiesta

The headmistress's speech will begin at 9 a.m.
Lessons will follow straightaway.

Signed,

Professor Snout

Professor Snout

Both Oscar and Arabella were looking forward to going back to the Academy, mainly because the new term would end in the fabulous Founder's Fiesta!

The Founder's Fiesta is one of THE most exciting days in the Mammoth Academy year. The whole Academy gets decorated with banners and balloons. Cook bakes enormous Founder's Fiesta desserts. There are no lessons and no uniforms, and there is plenty of feasting and dancing until very late at night.

EVERYONE was excited about it!

HONK!

On the first day back, Oscar and Arabella greeted the friendly Megaloceros who helped them across the glacier. As they walked across the icy plains, the sun was shining and they were both in high spirits.

Along the way, lots of their school pals joined them. There was plenty of friendly banter.

"Hey, Fox! Haven't seen you in ages! How are you doing?"

"I'm cool! How are you?"

"Look! There's Giant Sloth and Prunella!"

Prunella was Arabella's best friend at the Academy. She was also the smallest pupil in the whole school.

Arabella liked Prunella because she was fashionable and wore pretty bows. Prunella liked Arabella because she was clever and strong and would look after her in the busy school corridors.

"Hi there, Prunella!"

"Hi there, Arabella!"

Everyone was carrying a big bundle of paper, books, ink, and lots of things to be used to prepare for the Founder's Fiesta.

As more and more first years joined the procession, the level of excitement rose . . . until they arrived at the Mammoth Academy gates.

Then suddenly everyone went very quiet.

Woooooooooo...

2.
NEW LESSONS

This wasn't the welcome back to the Academy that anyone had been expecting.

As the school assembled to hear the headmistress give her "start the term" speech, you could have heard a pinecone drop.

"Welcome back, everyone," she began. "As you know, this term will end with the Founder's Fiesta. I had hoped to talk about it this morning, but it seems a more pressing matter has come up.

"You will have noticed that some unpleasant graffiti has appeared outside the school gates. We think that this could mean there are humans about!

"In case you've forgotten, this is what they look

like. They are wild and dangerous animals and are to be avoided! Take care when entering or leaving the school, stay close to your friends, and if anyone

sees anything suspicious, contact a member of the staff immediately.

"Now, here are your schedules. Off you go."

After that, they had lots of new lessons, including science with Dr. Van Der Graph.

"Right, everyone. Put on your safety goggles, your safety aprons, and your safety gloves.

"And now, start mixing things in test tubes...."

Fox's test tube turned brown.

Oscar's test tube turned orange.

But Arabella's test tube started to fizz and spit little silver sparks all over the place, finally going POOF! in a cloud of thick green smoke.

"Fascinating!" said Dr. Van Der Graph. "I think you have just made a scientific discovery!"

Next was dance class with Mrs. Waft. "This term we are going to learn a special dance to perform at the Founder's Fiesta," she told them. "I want you all to imagine you are tiny feathers floating on the breeze. . . ."

Last came art class with Professor Sable. "Hi! This term you're each going to make something AMAZING and INCREDIBLE with all the materials you have collected during the break. First I want you to sketch your ideas. You can do this on your own or in a group. Let's go!"

PRUNELLA'S IDEAS
Prunella's Beauty Parlor!!
Get pretty for the Founder's Fiesta with...
GIANT SLOTH FELL ASLEEP

ARABELLA'S SKETCHES
(SHE FILLED LOTS OF SHEETS)
The Mammoth Mammoth Idea!
TRUNK

HUGE mammoth sculpture

↑
FRAMEWORK
UNDERNEATH

*

OSCAR
DIDN'T
GET ON
VERY
WELL

OSCAR
WOZ ERE

And then—BONG! BONG! BONG!—the gong rang to tell everyone it was time to go home.

After the exciting day, Oscar, Arabella, and their friends had almost forgotten about the humans. But as they walked through the Academy gates to head home to the herds, they were quickly reminded that they must take extra care.

All the friends stayed very close together as they walked, and nobody said much. They were looking out for signs of trouble.

As they passed by the big forest, Prunella thought she heard a strange noise. "What's that?" she asked. But her voice was so quiet that nobody heard her.

Prunella didn't want to unnecessarily alarm anyone, so she didn't mention it again.

3.
TROUBLE BREWING

The next day, more graffiti had appeared on the Academy walls. Everyone agreed that this could only be the work of the Cave Skool humans.

"Look at the handwriting and the bad spelling," said Arabella. "It just *has* to be them."

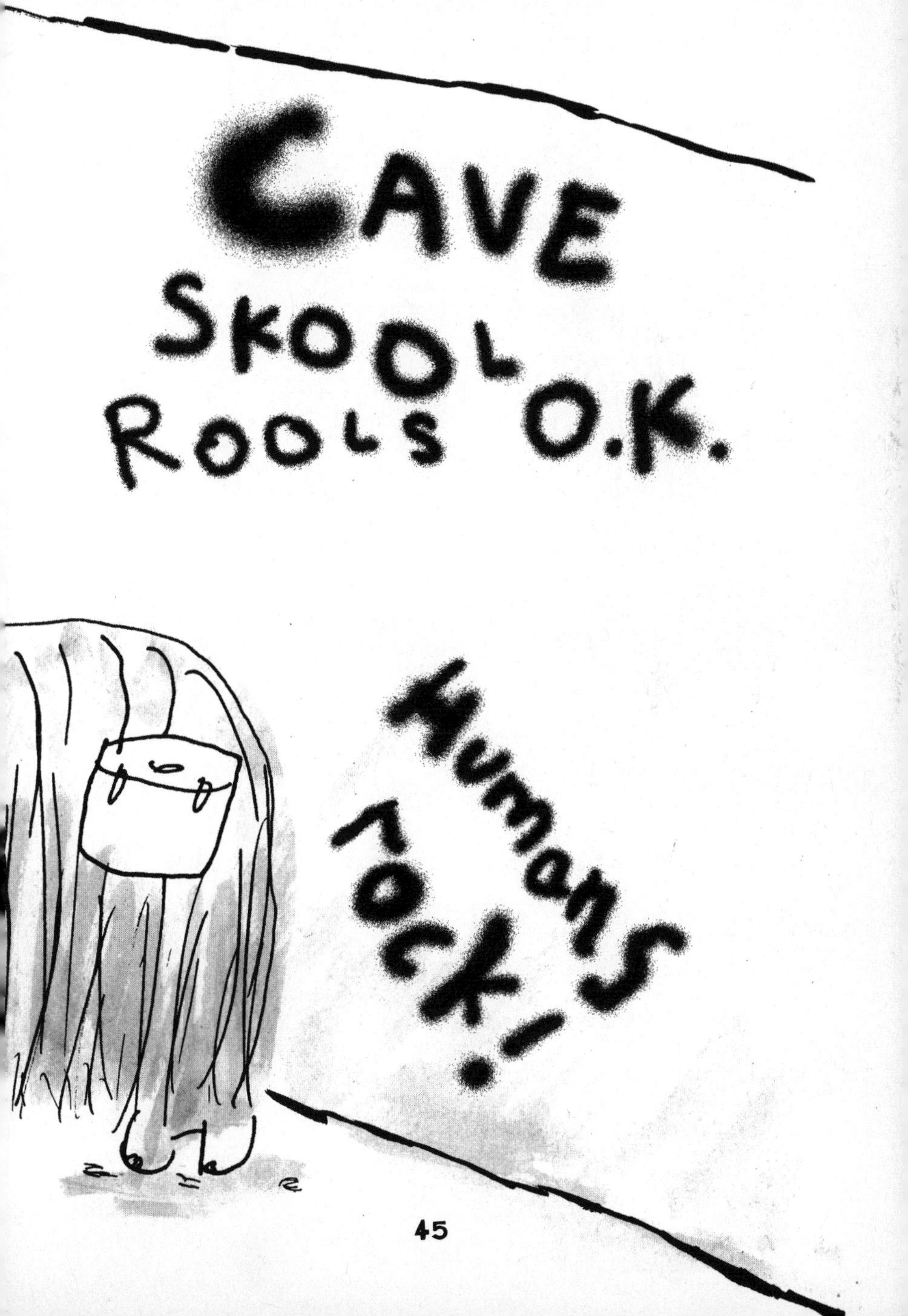
CAVE SKOOL ROOLS O.K.
Humans rock!

A window had been smashed in Cook's kitchen. Cook was not pleased. "If I ever get hold of the little savages, I'll show 'em what for!"

The news spread fast around the Academy, but there was nothing to do except carry on with business as usual.

That day's art lesson was spent working on the Founder's Fiesta projects.

Prunella constructed Prunella's Beauty Parlor, but with everyone so busy talking about the humans, nobody went to visit.

Arabella began working on the Mammoth Mammoth. Oscar's project wasn't going too well, so he asked if he could help. Arabella had just the job for him.

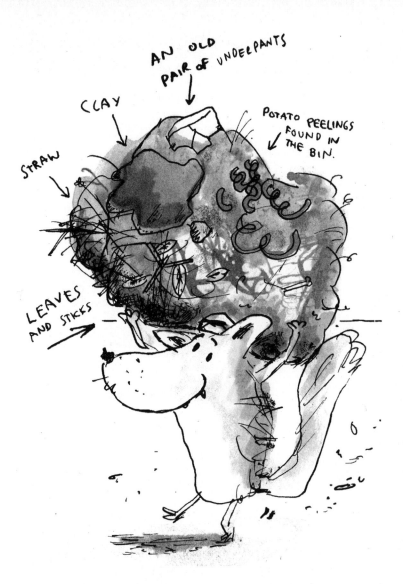

Fox thought the Mammoth Mammoth looked a
bit saggy, so he went off to find lots of things to
stuff it with.

The rabbits suggested that wheels and a rope might make it easy to parade about. And Prunella, after the unsuccessful opening of the beauty parlor, wondered if she could join in and pointed out that a few bows might make it look prettier. Owl and Giant Sloth were keen to help, too. In fact, by the end of the lesson, EVERYONE was involved in one way or another.

"This is going to be so cool when it's finished!" said Fox.

"Yeah!" Everyone agreed the class project was coming along very well indeed.

And suddenly—BONG! BONG! BONG!—it was time to go home again.

As the students walked through the graffiti-covered gates to the icy plains, they noticed more signs of human activity. The snow was littered with footprints, bits of rubbish, and the odd bit of dung.

"Urgh! How disgusting!" exclaimed Prunella.

They could definitely hear strange noises in the trees that seemed to go something like "Nah-nah, nah-nah!" and "Ugh!"

Oscar, Arabella, Prunella, Fox, and all their friends hurried homeward as fast as their legs would carry them.

4.
GIANT SLOTH

As the term carried on, something became apparent: The Cave Skool humans had moved into the area. There was more litter, dung, and noise, and a huge stone flag went up in the forest that read "CAVE SkOOL."

There was also more graffiti.

What should have been the BEST term of the year was now turning out to be the WORST.

Every day as the mammoths and their friends went to and from the Academy, the Cave Skool pupils would lurk in the woods, jeering and throwing snowballs.

The problem had gotten so bad that the friendly Megaloceros had to accompany the Mammoth Academy students all the way from the glacier right up to the school gates.

One day, when Oscar, Arabella, Prunella, and Giant Sloth went to go home, they found their path blocked.

Ahead on the icy plains stood a group of humans. "Ugh!" the humans said.

"I don't like the look of this," said Arabella.

"What shall we do?" squeaked Prunella.

"Heh heh UGH!" sniggered the humans.

And suddenly—THWACK!—something landed near Arabella's foot, and—FEEEEEEEE!—something whizzed toward Oscar, who just managed to hold up his school bag to deflect it.

"Ouch!" Oscar said. "That wasn't a snowball, that was an *ice* ball! Quick! Run for it!"

But before they could run anywhere—
THWACK!—a third, much larger ice ball hit Giant
Sloth squarely in the face.

Giant Sloth let out a deafening howl and waved his arms. His eyes, normally half shut, became as wide as saucers, and all his fur stood on end. He was obviously very, VERY angry!

The Cave Skool humans dropped their half-finished ice balls, turned tail, and ran scrambling and howling back up the mountain into the woods.

5.

THE SPARKLEBANG CODE

News of Giant Sloth's heroism went round the school fast. Students waved and cheered as he passed in the corridors, and teachers let him sit quietly at the back of the class and rest.

Everyone hoped that this might be the end of

the Cave Skool and that it would move away from the Academy and never be heard from again.

With the humans out of the way for the time being, life at the Academy began to go much better.

The caretaker managed to clean up the litter, scrub away the graffiti outside the gates, and replace the broken window. The students could walk to and from the Academy without worry, and everyone could carry on preparing for the fast-approaching Founder's Fiesta.

Arabella, under the guidance of Dr. Van Der Graph, had made hundreds more discoveries . . .

. . . and found that glorious things happened when certain mixtures were heated.

This prompted Dr. Van Der Graph to write a
code of use for all sparklebang mixtures.

THE SPARKLEBANG CODE

All sparklebang mixtures must
be kept in a sealed box or tin.

All sparklebang mixtures must
be kept away from hot things.

Always wear safety gear.

Sparklebang mixtures can be
dangerous and must only be
used with the supervision of a
responsible adult.

Signed,

Dr Van der Graph

Then Fox had another one of his great ideas. "Hey! Why don't we add some sparklebang mixtures to the Mammoth Mammoth? We could parade it about at the fiesta and then at the end of the evening start it sparkling. It would look amazing spitting and fizzing at night!"

Everyone agreed this was a splendid idea, and so Dr. Van Der Graph began joining in the art lessons, making special mixtures with Arabella and placing them carefully inside the Mammoth Mammoth.

Mrs. Waft had also taken to spending her time in the art room, saying it would give her inspiration for the special Founder's Fiesta dance she was creating.

In fact, everything was going really well . . . until the day the storm arrived.

It started with a gray sky and a few wispy flakes of snow, but by lunchtime, the sky had turned black. The snow began falling so heavily that it was impossible for the mammoths to see their trunks in front of their faces. Students crossing the court-yards had to shuffle along carefully in long lines,

each holding the tail in front. The sharp wind blowing from the icy plains caused huge snowdrifts to pile up against the walls and windows of the Academy.

By late afternoon the storm was at its height. None of the mammoth teachers could remember weather this bad, and some of them had very long memories indeed.

It was decided that sending the students home in such terrible weather would be unwise, so everyone had to spend the night in the Academy.

The gates were closed, and lots of blankets and sheets were brought down to the gymnasium so that it could act as a temporary sleeping area for students and staff. Ormsby said that the gym mats smelled of cheesy feet and that he wasn't keen to sleep on them, but nobody listened to his complaints.

Cook gave out hot soup, and everyone tried to bed down and get some sleep, while outside the storm raged on.

For the first few days, staying overnight in the Academy was quite fun, rather like a camping trip or a sleepover at a friend's burrow. But everyone was relieved when, after several days and nights, the wind began to drop.

Most of the lower windows were completely covered with snow and ice, but from the higher windows the animals could peer out and survey the weather. Some of the students thought they saw dark shapes moving outside, and some heard strange noises.

"There are lots of animals out there!" exclaimed Fox.

"I think they are HUMANS!" shouted Oscar.

6.
SURROUNDED!

"Please remain calm," said the headmistress. "It seems that we are surrounded. All students will remain here until help arrives. Once the weather clears, it shouldn't be too long."

But it kept snowing.

The staff and pupils tried to carry on with

lessons as normal. They had to rush on to the roof every now and then and throw a few hundred snowballs to keep the humans at bay.

Outside, Cave Skool lessons seemed to be continuing as well.

And still it kept snowing. Days passed. Oscar, Arabella, and their friends missed the herds and got more and more anxious.

And then, with Cook unable to go shopping, food started to run out. All that was left were wheat-husk crackers and cabbage. And though Cook did her best to be creative, her recipes were not the most appetizing of foods to eat for breakfast, lunch, *and* dinner.

Toilet paper was getting low, too. Professor
Snout allowed each pupil three sheets a day, which
is not very much at all.

A few days later, the tusk paste ran out, so everybody had cabbagy breath.

Outside the Academy walls, the Cave Skool seemed to be forming a plan.

Inside the Academy, the animals were worried and scared.

And then the scratching started. Nobody was sure who got them first, but the cause of the problem was clear: FLEAS!

The entire Academy was crawling with them!

Everyone was in a very disheveled and miserable state. Even Fox, who normally enjoyed being disheveled, hung his head in dismay and looked at the floor.

"We're doomed!" moaned one mammoth.

"It's the end! The end of the Mammoth Academy and the end of us!" whispered another.

"There's no hope," mumbled a third.

Suddenly, everyone heard a loud "HEY!" They looked around to see who was speaking.

It was Prunella. She had climbed right up to the
top of the Mammoth Mammoth and was shouting
at the top of her voice through a rolled-up piece of
paper.

"HEY!" she shouted again. "That attitude

simply isn't good enough! I may be the smallest one in the Academy, but there is no way that I am giving up, and you can't either!

"Have you all forgotten that the Founder's Fiesta is TONIGHT? Well, I am not going to have it ruined by some silly humans!

"We need to pull together. We can beat the humans! We can beat the hunger! And we can beat the fleas!

"Whoever comes to my beauty parlor will get their fleas combed out and a free new fur-style as well!"

7.
TEAMWORK

The line for Prunella's Beauty Parlor went twice around the great hall, but somehow Prunella managed to keep up with demand.

Briskly brushing, quickly combing and clipping,

she removed fleas from animal after animal and
gave them all snappy new styles.

All the grooming was generating huge amounts of fluff, and Arabella had just the use for it. "It lends the Mammoth Mammoth such a realistic air, don't you think?"

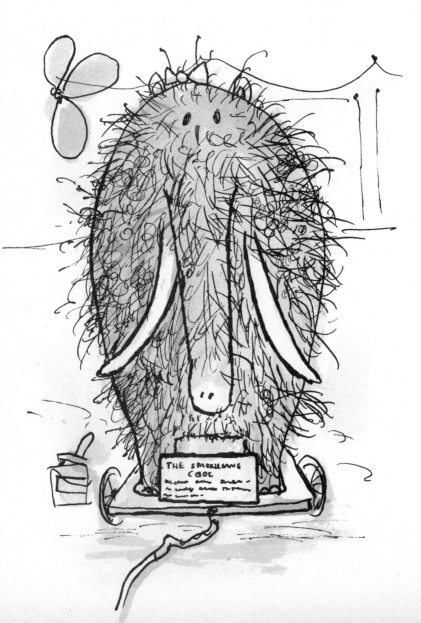

Finally, with everyone working together, the banners were hung, the tables were set, and the amazing and incredible Mammoth Mammoth was ready for the Founder's Fiesta parade!

Suddenly, the special alarm gong was sounded.

"THE HUMANS HAVE ENTERED THE ACADEMY! Quick! Everyone to the emergency escape tunnel!" cried the headmistress.

8.

THE MAMMOTH MAMMOTH

The teachers rushed all the pupils down corridors, across courtyards, and into the secret emergency escape tunnel. It was very dusty and very dark, but there was no other choice. The mammoths stumbled along blindly, following the

twists and turns, climbing stair after stair, until they eventually emerged onto a small ledge half-way up the mountain.

THE ESCAPE TUNNEL

The small ledge

Meanwhile, inside the Academy, the humans were going berserk, jumping on tables, throwing bits of paper about, and knocking over bookshelves.

They turned Cook's kitchen upside down, scattering jars, smashing plates, splintering cupboards, and eating vast quantities of wheat-husk crackers and cabbage.

And then they found the Mammoth Mammoth. For a few seconds they stared at it in awe. They had never seen anything like it. It was the biggest mammoth they had ever seen—or, as they thought, the biggest DINNER they had ever seen.

"FOOOOOOOOOD!"

"YUMMMMM!"

Forming a circle around it, they began shouting "Ugh!" and waving their spears and clubs.

The Mammoth Mammoth stared calmly back at them.

Then they began waving their spears and clubs more vigorously and shouting "Ugh!" a bit louder.

The Mammoth Mammoth continued staring calmly.

With confidence growing, one of them threw a spear at the Mammoth Mammoth. THOCK! The spear landed quivering in its side. More spears followed, and ice balls, and rocks, and books, and anything else that came to hand. After several more direct hits, a bit of its ear came off, and its head began to slump to one side.

A great cheer went up from the humans. Their prey had been defeated! FOOD!

Professor Ugh advanced toward the Mammoth Mammoth. He grabbed the Sparklebang Code stuck carefully to the front of the trolley and put it in his mouth. It obviously didn't taste very nice because he spat it out.

Then he took a bite of the Mammoth Mammoth's leg. This seemed to taste better.

After realizing it was too big to push on his own, he ordered the smaller humans to help him by pulling the two ropes handily attached to the front. They began wheeling it out of the great hall, through the gates, and toward their makeshift camp outside the Academy walls.

They couldn't wait to start feasting upon it.

Huddled on the mountain ledge,
the mammoths and their friends
looked on with interest.

9.
AT LAST!

The humans wheeled the Mammoth Mammoth to their campfire and stoked the flames. Then they began to pluck and shave the mammoth's wool.

"I can't believe they're doing that after all our hard work!" exclaimed Ormsby.

"I think they're going to try to cook it," said Arabella.

"In that case, I'm glad we're up here and they're down there," said Dr. Van Der Graph.

By now the humans had managed to man-handle the huge object onto an enormous spit over the fire. About six small humans hung from a handle at one end and rotated it gently while the rest of the humans looked on hungrily.

"I really do think they ought to have read the Sparklebang Code," said Dr. Van Der Graph.

"Look! Its tail is starting to sizzle," said Oscar.

"It's only a matter of time now," said Prunella.

All of a sudden, as the Mammoth Mammoth rotated on the spit, a beautiful shower of tiny silver stars poured out of its ears.

"Ooooooooooooo!" A ripple of approval

went through the crowd of mammoths on the mountain.

The Mammoth Mammoth spun faster and faster, launching humans in all directions, as the stars changed from silver to gold to pink.

"Mmmmmmmmmm!" murmured the crowd of mammoths.

"UGH?!" yelled the humans.

Suddenly—POP! POP! POP!—shimmering
bunches of brightly colored flowers shot high
into the sky and gently drizzled down to earth as

the Mammoth Mammoth spun even faster.

"Ahhhhhhhhhhh!" exclaimed the mammoths on the mountain.

"UGHHHH?!" cried the Cave Skool huma

"I called that one Alpine Glade," said Araber

"And now comes my most potent creation—
Armageddon!"

moth Mammoth was spinning
the blur of vibrant colors getting
iter and brighter and brighter

It exploded in a stunning display of every single color you could possibly imagine.

"BRAVO!" The mammoths on the mountain applauded. "Well done!"

"UGHHHHHH!!!!!" squealed the humans, who were running in all directions and doing anything they could to get as far away as possible from the flaming, hissing, spitting Mammoth Mammoth monster.

One of the humans' fur hats had caught fire, and everyone agreed that the effect was quite remarkable.

Just then there was a HOOT HOOT HOOT HOOOOT, and over the horizon appeared a horde of very big, furry animals.

"It's the herds!" exclaimed the mammoths on the mountain. "They've come to rescue us!"

The herds charged.

"You've been scaring my kids!" shouted one angry mother.

"Nobody upsets my young 'uns!" shouted another.

The humans turned and ran as fast as their legs could carry them. Up through the forests and over the mountains they went, never to been seen in mammothdom again.

UGH!

The animals carefully made their way down from the mountain. Mammoths, owls, giant sloths, cave bears, foxes, rabbits, and rodents were reunited with their mothers, fathers, brothers, and sisters. And everyone was glad that all were safe and sound.

"After that stupendous display, I think it's time to begin the Founder's Fiesta!" announced the headmistress.

And they did.

The herds had brought vast quantities of food with them. "We thought you might be hungry," they said.

The tables were groaning under the weight. Cook quickly rustled up some enormous Founder's Fiesta puddings and blackberry juice. And so began one of the most memorable Founder's Fiestas ever.

There was dancing, including Mrs. Waft's
special Founder's Fiesta flamenco.

There were party games. There was feasting. There was trumpeting.

There was everything you could ever want from a party, and more!

10.
FINALLY

And so another Mammoth Academy term ended.

The celebrating continued long into the night and way past everyone's bedtime. The stories of Arabella's magical exploding Mammoth Mammoth, Prunella's bravery, and the events leading

up to it were told for many, many mammoth years to come.

And they all got top marks for their projects.

THE REALLY, REALLY HIGH MOUNTAINS
CAVE SKOOL
THE CLIFFS
THE MARSHY MARSH
THE WILD LANDS
N
E
W
S
THE ICY PLAINS

THE MAMMOTH
ACADEMY

THE ICE
LAKE

THE
HERDS →

THE ALMOST IMPOSSIBLE
TO CROSS GREAT GLACIER

MAP OF THE
MAMMOTH
LANDS

THE
END